Adventures in Literacy

# Sixteen Fleecy Sheep

## a book about vowels

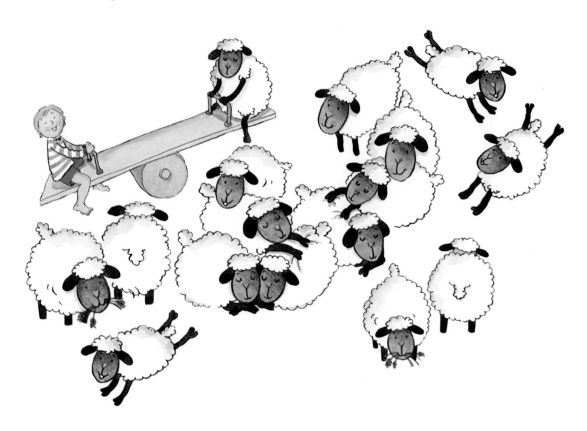

Ruth Thomson

Thameside Press

Distributed in the United States by
Smart Apple Media
1980 Lookout Drive
North Mankato, MN 56003

ISBN 1-930643-61-6

Library of Congress Control Number: 2001088834

Series editors: Mary-Jane Wilkins, Stephanie Turnbull
Designers: Rachel Hamdi, Angie Allison
Illustrators: Louise Comfort, Charlotte Hard, Holly Mann
Educational consultants: Pie Corbett, Poet and Consultant
    to the English National Literacy Strategy;
    Sarah Mullen, Literacy Consultant

Printed in Hong Kong

9  8  7  6  5  4  3  2  1

# Sixteen Fleecy Sheep

## a book about vowels

This beautiful book will help lay the early foundations for reading. Young children love words and often invent their own, savoring the sounds. They will enjoy having the rhymes and sentences read to them, and spotting objects in the pictures that contain the same sound.

Each page introduces a certain sound, so that children become aware of the different sounds that letters make. Early play with sounds, rhymes, and letters is fun and a fundamental beginning to becoming a reader.

Children are never too young to enjoy words, letters, and sounds. They make the pathway to reading both simple and joyful.

*Pie Corbett*

**Pie Corbett**
**Poet and Consultant to the**
**English National Literacy Strategy**

Pages 29 and 30 focus on the sounds "ee" and "ay" and the various spellings for each. Once children have learned to recognize each sound, they can move on to identifying it in its various forms.
A list of words illustrated in the book follows on pages 31 and 32.

# ee

Sixteen fleecy sheep
asleep in the street.

# ee

sheep

jeep

feet

wheel

bee

seed

reed

weed

sheet

What insects can you see?
What is hanging on the clothesline?

4

**ea**

The beastly weasel steals ice cream from the feast.

**ea**

weasel

peach

beads

easel

eagle

teapot

seal

peas

leaf

beaver

What food is there at the feast?
What animals can you see?

**ai**

mermaid

# The vain mermaid waits for the sailors in the rain.

**ai**

mermaid

sailor

rail

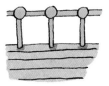
paintbrush

rain

nail

sail

paint

tail

snail

What are the sailors doing?
What can you see that is red?

6

ay ay

# "It's our birthday today!" say May and Fay.

birthday cake

crayon

clay

tray

hay

Where is the hamster hiding?
What day of the week is it?

# a-e

ape

plate

grapes

snake

skate

## Jake the ape waves to Kate from his cave.

Jake's Cave

For Sale

# a-e

cave

gate

cage

game

cake

What is Kate carrying?
What are the animals going to eat?

8

# Five white mice ride their bikes for miles.

mice

hive

kite

pine

5

five

bike

fire

knife

line

vine

What is the man holding?

What is the boy doing?

# o-e

# o-e

The gnome pokes the mole on the nose.

mole

stove

stone

rope

cone

gnome

nose

smoke

hose

bone

What is on the mole's table?
What is hanging on the wall?

u-e

# The duke played Luke a tune on his flute.

u-e

duke

flute

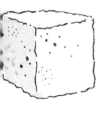

cube

tube

chute

prune

What are the boys throwing?

What can you see in the background?

# igh

**The lightning frightens the fighting knights.**

# igh

knight

lightning

light

tights

night

midnight

fight

What are the pages holding?

What time is it?

# oa

The boastful toad has a boat and a coach.

## oa

coach

loaf

boat

cloak

oak

toad

soap

road

goat

foam

What is the coachman doing?
What is the toad eating?

# OW

crows

rainbow

bow

arrow

## The crows follow the farmer's wheelbarrow.

# OW

scarecrow

window

pillow

What is standing in the field?
What can you see in the sky?

# The moose and the goose run loose at the zoo.

baboon

stool

bamboo

goose

spoon

pool

broom

kangaroo

balloon

What are the baboons holding?
What other animals can you see?

# ew

A few newts wore new jewelry to dinner.

newt

newspaper

jewelry

yew

# ew

stew

screw

screwdriver

What are the newts eating?
What can you see outside?

# "Who took my book?" said the angry cook.

cook

foot

hook

hood

wood

cookbook

wool

wood

What is on the table?
What can you see outside?

# ar

The gu**ar**d dog b**ar**ks in al**ar**m at the sp**ar**ks.

farmer

guitar

arch

harness

jar

# ar

car

barn

cart

scarf

garden

What is the farmer holding?
What can you see in the yard?

"How now, brown cow?"
growls the clown.

OW

OW

clown

owl

cauliflower

town

crown

tower

sunflower

cow

What is the clown holding?
Who is sitting in the tree?

19

# OU

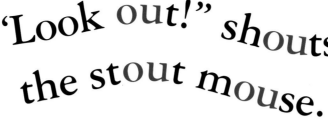

"Look out!" shouts the stout mouse.

 mountain

 mouse

 cloud

 fairground

 house

 flour

 fountain

 Brussels sprout

spout

What are all the mice doing?
What can you see through the window?

# "Where are my eclairs?" sighed the millionaire.

millionaire

rocking chair

hairbrush

eclair

highchair

wheelchair

stairs

What kinds of chair can you see?
What is on the table?

ea

"Treasure! We're wealthy!" yelled the dreadful pirates.

ea

head

bread

heavy

sweater

feather

pheasant

treasure

weapons

What is one pirate eating?
What bird can you see?

ear

Two fat bears sat guzzling juicy pears.

ear

bear

underwear

pear

Clare was scared by a hare in her nightmare.

are

are

hare

square

# or

A tortoise and a stork crossed swords in the fort.

## or

stork

fort

shorts

sword

fork

thorn

horse

recorder

What are the children doing?
What animals can you see?

aw

aw

The sprawling lion woke at dawn and yawned.

hawk

shawl

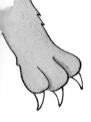
claw

drawing

paw

strawberry

dawn

straw

What is the girl going to eat?
What is the baby doing?

## "Oh no, don't squirt!" says the girl in the skirt.

girl

fir

shirt

bird

skirt

dirty

What is the girl wearing?
What are the boy's pants like?

# The turtles twist and turn on purple surfboards.

turtle

surfboard

purse

burger

nurse

surf

turnip

turkey

Burger Bar

Who is helping the hurt turtle?
What food can you see?

**er**

# The eager beaver scampers over the river.

tiger

beaver

panther

river

banner

**er**

otter

hamster

tower

ladder

Who is coming down the slide on the tower?

Who is watching him?

# Steve shrieks at the geese feeding in the field.

jeans

leaf

peach

peas

cheese

geese

sheep

tree

key

field

Listen to the ee sounds in the sentence.

Can you find more ee sounds in the picture?

# a-e          ai          ay

## Kay the mermaid played in the spray with the whale.

cape

whale

mermaid

rail

sail

sailor

tail

spray

Listen to the ay sounds in the sentence.
Look for more ay sounds in the picture.

# Word list

Here are all the words illustrated in this book.

## a-e
(p. 8)

ape
cage
cake
cave
crate
date
game
gate
grape
Jake
Kate
mane
name
plate
sale
shade
skate
snake
suitcase
wave

## ai
(p. 6)

bait
chain
mermaid
nail
pain
paint
paintbrush
rail
rain
sail
sailboat
sailor
snail

tail
vain
wait

## air
(p. 21)

armchair
chair
despair
eclair
hair
hairbrush
highchair
millionaire
pair
repair
repairman
rocking
  chair
stairs
wheelchair

## ar
(p. 8)

ajar
alarm
arch
arm
bark
barn
barnyard
car
cardigan
carpet
cart
carton
dart
dartboard

farm
farmer
farmhouse
garden
garlic
guard dog
guitar
harness
jar
marmalade
scarf
spark
yard

## are
(p. 23)

bare
Clare
hare
nightmare
scare
square

## aw
(p. 25)

claw
crawl
dawn
draw
drawing
gnaw
hawk
paw
shawl
sprawl
straw
strawberry
yawn

## ay
(p. 7)

birthday
birthday
  cake
clay
crayon
display
Fay
Friday
hay
May
Monday
play
Thursday
today
tray
Tuesday
Saturday
Sunday
Wednesday

## ea
(p. 5)

beach
bead
beak
beastly
beaver
eagle
easel
eat
feast
greasy
heap
heat
ice cream
leaf

lean
meal
meat
pea
peach
reach
read
sea
seal
seashore
squeak
squeal
steal
tea
teach
teacup
teapot
weasel
wreath

## ea
(p. 22)

bread
dreadful
feather
forehead
head
heavy
leather
meadow
measure
pheasant
pleasure
redhead
spread
sweat
sweater
treasure
wealthy
weapon

## ear
(p. 23)

bear
pear
underwear

## ee
(p. 4)

asleep
bee
feed
feet
fleecy
jeep
reed
seed
sheep
sheet
sixteen
sleep
street
sweep
sweeper
weed
weep
wheel

## ew
(p. 16)

chew
few
jewelry
new
newspaper
newt
screw
screwdriver
stew
yew

## i-e
(p. 9)

bike
bite
fire
five
hive
kite
knife
lime
line
mice
mile
pine
rice
ride
ripe
rise
side by
  side
smile
stripe
vine
white
wide
wife
wipe

## igh
(p. 12)

bright
fight
frighten
high
knight
light
lightning
midnight
night
right
tights

## ir
(p. 26)

birch
bird
chirp
dirty
fir
girl
shirt
skirt
squirt
swirl
twirl

## oa
(p. 13)

boastful
boat
cloak
coach
coachman
coat
float
foam
goat
loaf
moat
oak
road
soap
toad

## o-e
(p. 10)

bone
cone
doze
gnome
hole
home
hose

joke
mole
nose
phone
poke
rope
rose
slope
smoke
stone
stove

## oo
(p. 15)

baboon
balloon
bamboo
broom
cockatoo
goose
kangaroo
loose
moose
pool
raccoon
scooter
snooze
spoon
stool
zoo
zookeeper

## oo
(p. 17)

book
cook
cookbook
foot
hood
hook
took

wood
wooden
wool
woolly

## or
(p. 24)

corner
fork
fort
horse
popcorn
recorder
short
shorts
stork
story
sword
thorn
torn
tortoise
uniform

## ou
(p. 20)

bounce
Brussels
  sprout
cloud
counter
fairground
flour
fountain
house
mound
mountain
mouse
mouth
out
outside
pounce

shout
spout
stout

## ow
(p. 14)

arrow
blow
bow
bungalow
crow
elbow
flow
follow
furrow
narrow
pillow
rainbow
row
scarecrow
shadow
swallow
wheelbarrow
window
yellow

## ow
(p. 19)

bow
brown
cauliflower
clown
cow
crowd
crown
flower
frown
growl
how
howl
now

owl
scowl
sunflower
tower
town

## u-e
(p. 11)

amuse
chute
cube
duke
dune
flute
Luke
prune
rude
tube
tune

## ur
(p. 27)

burger
burn
curly
furry
hurt
nurse
purple
purse
surf
surfboard
surfer
turkey
turn
turnip
turtle